SECRET of the GHOST PIANO

Written by Elizabeth Bolton

Illustrated by Gioia Fiammenghi

Troll Associates

Library of Congress Cataloging in Publication Data

Bolton, Elilzabeth.
    Secret of the ghost piano.

    Summary: Two boys spending the night together hear
mysterious piano music in the middle of the night.
    1. Children's stories, American. [1. Mystery and
detective stories] I. Fiammenghi, Gioia, ill. II. Title.
PZ7.B63597Se   1985   [E]   84-8745
ISBN 0-8167-0410-4 (lib. bdg.)
ISBN 0-8167-0411-2 (pbk.)

10 9 8 7 6 5 4 3 2 1

SECRET of the GHOST PIANO

"Don't forget your toothbrush, Jim," Mom said. "Don't stay up too late. Don't ask for things to eat. And *please* don't tease the sitter." Those were an awful lot of don'ts.

I was going to sleep over with my friend Tom that night. Our folks were going out together. That's why we had to have a baby sitter at Tom's. I think I'm too old for sitters. Mom *doesn't* think so.

"Have you got your sleeping bag?" Mom asked. "Do you want to take some games?" She acted like I was going away for a week.

It was Friday afternoon. I was going to have dinner at Tom's house. Tom and I

planned lots of things to do. But Mom was still thinking up new things *not* to do. "Don't tease to watch late TV," she said. "And I don't want you watching the scary movie that's on tonight!"

I didn't tell Mom I *liked* being scared.
She wouldn't want to hear it. I also didn't
ask, "Can I take George with me?" George is
my hamster. If I did ask, Mom would just say
no. So I wrapped George's cage up tight in
my sleeping bag.

Mom was putting on her jacket. "Are you ready, Jim?" she asked. "Have you got everything? Why is your sleeping bag so lumpy?"

Just in time, Dad burst in. Was I glad to see him! "Come on, you two!" he said. "We're late!" He rushed me and my sleeping bag out to the car. We all drove over to Tom's house.

The baby sitter was already there. "This is Lisa," Tom's mom said. "She'll give you dinner. And she knows how late you can stay up." Tom rolled his eyes at me. His dad saw it and grinned.

"You'll survive," he said. "Come on, folks. Let's get going." The grownups left.

Lisa smiled at us. "Dinner is in five minutes, guys. Go wash your hands."

Tom grabbed my duffel bag and raced upstairs. I grabbed the sleeping bag and raced up, too.

Tom's house is pretty old, and his room is great. It has a high ceiling and a rounded tower in the corner. Tom's big orange hamster, Sam, was in a cage near the window.

"We can sleep any place you want," Tom said. "We could sleep on the beds. Or we could put our sleeping bags on the floor." I could tell that was what he wanted to do.

Then Tom's eyes got big. "Hey, your sleeping bag's making a noise!"

"George!" I said. "I almost forgot."

I undid the sleeping bag and took out the cage. George stood on his hind legs and wrinkled his nose at us.

"Boys!" Lisa shouted up the stairs. "The spaghetti's getting cold!"

We took George and Sam down with us. Lisa pulled a chair up next to ours. "The cages can stay on that," she said. So George and Sam wriggled around and watched us eat. I sneaked them some spaghetti. So did Tom. Lisa caught us but she didn't get mad. She gave me two helpings without me even hinting.

"Lisa's okay, for a girl," Tom admitted.

"Oh, really?" Lisa smiled. "Who beat you at arm wrestling last week? And who took you to see that ghost movie for your birthday?"

"Ghost movie!" I said. "I didn't know you liked ghost stories!"

"I'll say!" Tom grinned. "I've got twenty-three ghost books upstairs. And do you know what?" He leaned over and whispered. *"This house is haunted!"*

I stared at him. "It's not!"

"It is! Cross my heart," said Tom. "My grandpa lived here when he was a little boy. He said there were ghosts in the attic. They came downstairs when people were asleep. Once he heard a ghost play the piano in the middle of the night."

"Don't make up stories," Lisa said.

"I'm not making it up," Tom said. "My grandpa heard it. He told me this was a ghost meeting place—a clubhouse. He says ghosts got together here to wail and moan on rainy nights."

Suddenly a clap of thunder sounded outside. It began to rain. I looked at Tom. He
winked at me.

"I bet the ghosts will come tonight," I said and poked Tom in the ribs.

Tom poked me back. "I bet they're going to moan all night. This is how they sound. *W-O-O-O-O-O!*"

He twirled around the kitchen waving his arms. So did I. We both laughed.

"Oh, brother!" Lisa groaned. "You guys can play for an hour. Then get ready for bed."

Tom and I played with George and Sam
in the living room. We let them out of their
cages to play hide-and-seek. We made up a
ghost story about Tom's house. We told it
loudly so Lisa could hear it. She acted like she

didn't notice. But every so often, she went to
the window and looked outside. It was
raining hard now. The wind whistled in the
chimney. I wondered whether Tom's
grandpa's ghosts really *might* come that night.

When it was almost time for bed, Tom remembered there was cake in the kitchen. So we had cake and milk. Tom sat at the piano and pretended to be a ghost. *"Eee-ooo-eee-ooo!"* he wailed. He plinked at the piano keys, splashed his milk, and scattered lots of cake crumbs.

"Okay," said Lisa, "this is how ghosts scare kids to bed. GGGGGOOOOOO!" Lisa chased us to the stairs. We went up them, moaning and waving our arms. It was pretty silly. We wailed ourselves to Tom's room and rolled on the floor, laughing.

I don't know when we got to sleep. It wasn't early. But I *do* know when I woke up.

It was raining outside and the house was completely dark. Lisa had gone. Tom's mom and dad were home asleep. Downstairs, some-body was playing the piano.

Suddenly I was wide awake. Somebody

was *playing the piano* in the middle of the
night! And it didn't sound like the way
normal people play.   DUM.   DA.
DUM.   *PLONKKK.*

   I lay in my sleeping bag, almost too scared
to breathe. All I could think of was Tom's
story about the ghosts.

"Jim?" I almost jumped a mile. It was
Tom's voice, whispering to me.
"Yeah?"
"Do you hear that?" he asked.

"*Yeah.*" I *wasn't* imagining it, then. We could barely see each other in the moonlight. Tom's face looked white.

DUM.   DA.   *DUM*.

Tom and I crawled out of our sleeping
bags. We didn't say a word. We tiptoed to the
closed door. We opened it a crack.   DUM.
DUM.

Tom was really brave. He tiptoed to the stairs and down one step. The piano kept playing. He went down another step. *Creak!*
Suddenly the playing stopped. We froze. Outside the window the trees in the moon-

light looked like gray skeletons.   DUM.
DA.   *DUM.*   DUM.   DA.
   Now it sounded like two playing at once!
What had Tom said about a ghosts' club
meeting?   DUM.   DE-*DUMMMMMM!*

Suddenly we heard a sound behind us. It was a door opening!

Luckily, it was Tom's dad in the hall. He had a flashlight but it wasn't lit. He looked at us and put a finger to his lips.

He tiptoed downstairs. We tiptoed as quietly and as slowly as possible.

The weird piano playing continued. Now we were in the downstairs hall, in the archway to the living room.

DA.   DA.   *PLONKKK.*

The piano was just around the corner.

Wham! Tom's dad turned the flashlight on and aimed it straight at the piano. Something froze. Something sat up. *Two* things. One was brown and furry. One was furry and orange.

"*George!*" I cried.

"*Sam!*" Tom dove for the piano. The hamster leaped onto his arm. George sat on his hind legs and wrinkled his nose at me.

"How did they get out of their cages?" Tom's
dad asked.

All at once I remembered. Tom and I must have forgotten to put them back in their cages after we ate our cake!

But before I could say a word, Tom grabbed my arm. "I'll bet Sam opened the cages!" he said. "Sam can do anything. Can't you, Sam? You can even play the piano!"

Tom's dad laughed. Then he looked at the piano. "Somebody was eating cake at the piano! Those hamsters aren't music lovers. They're *food* lovers!"

That was what Sam and George had been doing. They were jumping on the piano keys to get the cake crumbs!

Tom and I slept over together a lot after that. But from then on we remembered to put George and Sam back in their cages. And that was the last time we ever heard ghosts play the piano!

DA.   DA.   *PLONKKK.*